CTW
SESAME STREET®

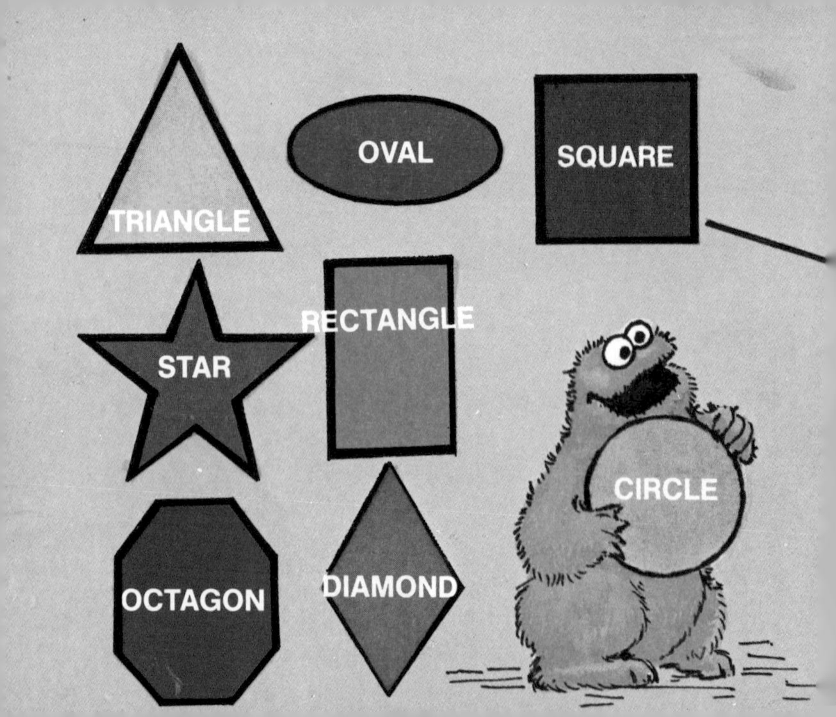
TRIANGLE
OVAL
SQUARE
STAR
RECTANGLE
CIRCLE
OCTAGON
DIAMOND

BIG BIRD'S SHAPE BOOK

Published in the United States by Random House, Inc., New York, in conjunction with Children's Television Workshop, New York. This edition first published in Canada by Random House of Canada Limited, Toronto. ISBN 0-394-83263-9
Library of Congress Catalog Card Number 75-39343
Printed in Singapore
First American Edition 7 8 9 0

CTW
SESAME STREET
Me help!

Oh, look. That piece of pie is shaped just like a TRIANGLE.
HOOPER'S PIES

Me happy to hold it for you.

I'll bet Oscar has something in his junk pile that is shaped like a SQUARE.
Here it is!

Me carry that, too.

Gosh! There's a CIRCLE!

Oh, hi, Bert! Just what I need—a RECTANGLE.
FUN WITH OATMEAL
PIGEONS I HAVE KNOWN

Mmmm!

Look! Somebody's kite got caught in the tree. I'll use it for my DIAMOND shape.

That kite look delicious!

Oh, how lucky! This skateboard I am tripping on is shaped just like an OVAL!

Yes, very lucky.

I don't think Guy Smiley would mind if I borrowed his STAR!
GUY SMILEY

No, he not mind!

Oh, dear, Cookie. We've found everything but an octagon. Where will we ever find one?

8 yummy sides!

Look! Ernie has an OCTAGON—a stop sign.

STOP

STOP
Oh, goodie. Now I have all the shapes I need to make my wonderful work of art!

Uh-oh!

Isn't it beautiful, Cookie?
Very good taste!

STOP
SHAPE
MOBILE
GIFT OF
ARTIST
B. BIRD